W9-BRF-011

NICKELODEON

降去神通

AVATAR
THE LAST AIRBENDER

THE LOST SCROLLS: WATER

BY MICHAEL TEITELBAUM
ILLUSTRATED BY PATRICK SPAZIANTE
BASED ON SCREENPLAYS BY
MICHAEL DANTE DIMARTINO, BRYAN KONIETZKO,
IAN WILCOX, JOHN O'BRYAN, AND AARON EHASZ.

SIMON SPOTLIGHT/NICKELODEON
NEW YORK   LONDON   TORONTO   S

visit us at www.abdopublishing.com

Reinforced library bound edition published in 2008 by Spotlight, a division of ABDO Publishing Group, 8000 West 78th Street, Edina, Minnesota 55439. Published by agreement with Simon Spotlight, an imprint of Simon & Schuster Children's Publishing Division.

SIMON SPOTLIGHT

An imprint of Simon & Schuster Children's Publishing Division
1230 Avenue of the Americas, New York, NY 10020

Library of Congress Cataloging-in-Publication Data

This title was previously cataloged with the following information:

Teitelbaum , Michael.
  The lost scrolls: water / Michael Teitelbaum ; [edited by] Orli Zuravicky.
    p. cm. -- (Avatar)
  I. Avatar (Television program). II. Title. III. Series.

[Fic]--dc22   2006925118

ISBN-13: 978-1-59961-459-5 (reinforced library bound edition)
ISBN-10: 1-59961-459-6 (reinforced library bound edition)

All Spotlight books have reinforced library binding
and are manufactured in the United States of America.

Prologue

3

降去神通

IF YOU ARE READING THIS,
you have uncovered one of the four hidden scrolls I
have compiled about the world of Avatar. The scroll
you have found contains sacred stories, legends, and
facts that I have gathered so far about the proud
nation of the Water Tribes—its history, its culture, and
the great tales of its past and present. I hope that
this information will be as useful and intriguing to you
as it is to me. As a great friend of the Water Tribes,
I ask that you keep this scroll safe and share it only
with those you trust. Beware, for there are many
who wish to expose its secrets. . . .

Introduction

降去神通

Long ago, in a time of peace, the Avatar kept balance between the four nations of the world—the Water Tribes, the Earth Kingdom, the Fire Nation, and the Air Nomads. In these nations there are people who have mastered the ability to control their culture's native element, an art form known as bending. They call themselves Waterbenders, Earthbenders, Firebenders, and Airbenders—only the Avatar can manipulate all four elements. When an Avatar dies, his or her spirit is reborn into a bender of the next nation in the cycle of Water, Earth, Fire, and Air. This cycle provides a natural balance, keeping any one nation from growing more powerful than the others.

As you know, the four nations lived in peace for many generations. But all that changed one hundred years ago, when the Fire Nation attacked.

The leader of the Fire Nation at that time, the powerful Firebender known as Fire Lord Sozin, had secret ambitions to take over the world by conquering the other nations. When Avatar Roku died, knowing that the next Avatar would be a child who needed training and maturity before he or she grew powerful enough to oppose him, Fire Lord Sozin secretly began to build a fleet of massive ships and train an army of Firebenders and soldiers. Throughout the years the Fire Nation's armada grew strong while the other nations remained ignorant. Then, using the energy of a passing comet, Fire Lord Sozin attacked the Water, Air, and Earth nations at the same time.

Only the Avatar had the skills to stop the ruthless Fire Nation. But when the world needed him most, the Avatar did not appear. Following the natural cycle—since Avatar Roku was from the Fire Nation— the next Avatar would come from the Air Nation. Sozin's army wiped out all of the Air Nomads, so the Avatar could never return.

Or so the world believed.

The war has raged for one hundred years. The Air Nomads were believed to have all been wiped out. Most of the great cities of the Southern Water Tribe were destroyed. Many of the Earth Kingdom's cities were taken over by Fire Nation soldiers, and hope was beginning to fade from the world. . . .

Until the day the Avatar returned.

The Avatar Returns
LEGEND 1

My name is Katara. I'm a member of the Southern Water Tribe. I'm fourteen now. I was told that my mother died when I was eight during a Fire Nation attack on my village. Two years ago my father and the other men of my tribe journeyed to the Earth Kingdom to help in the fight against the Fire Nation. He left me and my older brother, Sokka, to help look after our tribe.

Some people believe that the cycle was broken and the Avatar was never reborn. But I always believed that somehow the Avatar would return to save the world.

Sokka and I were in our canoe, fishing among the ice floes.

"I'll show you how to catch a fish, Katara," Sokka bragged.

That's my brother. He thinks he can do everything better than anyone else! But I was born a Waterbender, and although I have no training, I can still make water do some pretty neat things . . . and I was not going to let Sokka catch the only fish that day! Using my Waterbending abilities, I shaped a bubble out of water and caught a fish inside it!

"Sokka, look!" I cried.

"Shh, Katara!" Sokka whispered. "You're gonna scare the fish away."

My brother can be so infuriating sometimes! The "great fisherman" wouldn't even bother to look at the fish I had caught!

Sokka lifted his spear to go after his fish and accidentally burst the water bubble, soaking himself and letting my fish get away.

"Why is it every time you play with magic water, I get soaked?" Sokka grumbled.

"It's not magic, it's Waterbending," I explained for the millionth time. "It's—"

"I know," Sokka interrupted. "It's an ancient art unique to our culture, blah, blah, blah!"

Like I said, Sokka thinks he knows everything.

Suddenly the current picked up, smashing our boat into a huge chunk of ice. Sokka couldn't control the boat, so we jumped onto a floating iceberg.

"Leave it to a girl to mess things up!" Sokka yelled.

He was blaming this on me? That did it! "You are the most sexist, immature . . ." I could hardly get the words out, I was so furious. I realized Sokka was giving me a frightened, wide-eyed look. I thought I had finally gotten through my brother's thick head. All of a sudden I heard a huge cracking noise from behind, then spun around in time to see that an enormous iceberg had been split in half!

"Your powers have gone from weird to freakish, Katara!" Sokka cried.

"You mean I did that?" I asked. I was stunned. Could I really be that powerful a Waterbender?

"Yup, you did that," Sokka replied. "Congratulations!"

Suddenly the iceberg began to glow. "Look!" I shouted. "There's a boy frozen in the ice. And some kind of huge creature. Sokka, that boy is alive!"

I began hacking away at the ice with Sokka's war club. Finally the iceberg cracked, sending a brilliant beam of light into the sky and releasing its prisoner. As Sokka and I hurried to the boy's side, the arrow-shaped tattoo on his head stopped glowing.

"How did you get into the ice?" Sokka asked as the boy's eyes opened. "And why aren't you frozen?"

"I'm not sure," the boy replied.

We were all startled by a loud grunt.

"Appa!" the strange boy shouted, jumping to his feet. "Are you all right, buddy?"

"What *is* that thing?" Sokka asked.

"This is Appa, my flying bison," the boy replied. "Do you guys live around here?"

"Don't answer that!" Sokka shouted to me. "You saw that beam of light. He could be trying to signal the Fire Nation!"

"The paranoid one here is my brother, Sokka," I said, rolling my eyes. Sokka could be so mistrusting. "What's your name?"

"I'm ... A-A-ACHOO!" The boy sneezed and flew ten feet into the air. "I'm Aang," he said as he floated back down.

"You're an Airbender!" I cried.

"I sure am," Aang said proudly. "You guys need a ride?"

After convincing Sokka that the boy was harmless, the three of us climbed up onto the giant bison. Appa had some trouble getting up in the air. Sokka was really rude—he doesn't believe anything he can't prove—but I knew Appa would fly. All it took was some patience . . . and a little faith.

"Appa's just tired," Aang told us. "After he rests, he'll fly. You'll see."

Appa paddled through the water, all the way to my village. There, we introduced Aang to our grandmother, Gran Gran, and the other people of the village.

"No one has seen an Airbender for one hundred years," Gran Gran said. "We thought they were extinct."

"Extinct?" Aang said, sounding worried.

That's when Sokka grabbed Aang's staff. "What kind of weapon is this?" Sokka asked.

"It's not a weapon," Aang explained, taking back his staff. "It's a glider for Airbending. It lets me control the air currents and fly around."

"You know, last time I checked, people couldn't fly," Sokka said.

"Well, check again!" Aang said.

Then he soared into the sky on his glider! It was amazing to see a real bender practicing his art. All the little kids in the village squealed with delight!

Suddenly Aang crashed into the watchtower Sokka had built and knocked it over!

"Great!" moaned Sokka when Aang had landed. "You're an Airbender; Katara's a Waterbender. Together you can waste time all day long!"

I think Sokka was a little jealous of all the attention Aang was getting. The kids in our tribe had always looked up to Sokka, but in a matter of seconds, Aang stole the show.

"You're a Waterbender?" Aang asked me.

"Sort of," I replied. "I've got no one to train me. I'm the only Waterbender in the Southern Water Tribe."

"What about the Northern Water Tribe?" Aang asked.

"It's all the way on the other side of the world," I exclaimed.

"Appa and I can take you to the North Pole!" Aang said excitedly. "You can find a Waterbending master there to teach you!"

Finding a real Waterbending master to train me was what I had wanted my whole life. Part of me was ready to say yes right away, but the thought of leaving home was scary. What about Gran Gran and the rest of our village? Could I just walk away from them?

"While you think it over," he said, "let's go penguin sledding!"

I've never had so much fun! We slid down a steep hill on a couple of penguins. But at the bottom we saw an old Fire Nation ship that had been there for years. I told Aang we're not allowed to go near it, but he didn't listen.

"Katara," he said, "if you want to be a bender, you have to let go of your fears."

Aang was right. For years I've been afraid afraid of that ship, afraid of the Fire Nation, afraid that I'd never be a true Waterbender. Yes, if I was to become a bender, I had to stop being afraid.

So I followed Aang onto the ship.

"This ship is a very bad memory for my people," I explained to Aang. "It's from the Fire Nation's first attack on us in the war."

"Okay. Back up," Aang said. "I've never seen any war."

How could anyone not know about the war? Unless they were stuck inside an iceberg for . . .

"Aang," I said, not believing what I was about to tell him, "I think you were in that iceberg for a hundred years! That's why you don't know about the war."

"That's impossible," Aang cried. "Do I look like a one-hundred-and-twelve-year-old man to you?"

"Think about it," I told him. "The war is a century old. You don't know about it because, somehow, you were in ice that whole time. It's the only explanation."

Aang dropped to the ground. He seemed stunned. "A hundred years . . . I can't believe it."

"Come on," I said, helping him to his feet. "Let's get out of here."

But on the way off the ship, we triggered a booby trap. A flare shot high into the sky and exploded.

Aang put his arm around my waist and Airbended us into the sky and away from the ship.

"I knew it!" yelled Sokka when we returned to the village. "You signaled the Fire Nation with that flare!"

I pleaded with Sokka, telling him that it wasn't Aang's fault. But Aang took the blame for me.

"Aha," Sokka cried. "The traitor confesses! The foreigner is banished from our village!"

"Aang is not our enemy!" I cried, but no one seemed to listen to me. I felt so helpless. Once Sokka gets something into his head, there's no changing his mind.

Gran Gran lowered her head. "Katara," she said softly but sternly. "Going onto that ship is forbidden! Now we are all in danger. Sokka is right. I think it would be best if the Airbender left our village."

And so Aang left. I wanted to go with him, but I couldn't. Family comes first. That's how Sokka and I were raised, and that's what I believe.

But that doesn't mean I wasn't furious! "There goes my one chance of becoming a Waterbender!" I shouted at Gran Gran. I was so sick of this whole war, of what had become of all of us. It was all so unfair. I had never raised my voice to my grandmother in my life. And yet there I was, screaming at the woman I loved most in the world.

Just then a huge Fire Nation ship landed on our shore. The flare must have brought them to us. Prince Zuko of the Fire Nation strode from his

ship and marched into our village as if he owned it. The people of my village trembled and ran for cover. I was scared too, though I did my best to hide it. Sokka bravely stepped forward to confront the prince, but I knew that he couldn't take on a ship full of Firebenders all by himself!

"Where are you hiding him?!" Zuko demanded. "Where is the Avatar?"

Sokka tried to fight Zuko, but my brother was no match for the prince's Firebending power. As Sokka battled the prince, I feared for my brother's life. I also realized that I was too quick to judge Sokka. All he ever wanted was to do was protect us. That's why he's so mistrusting of others.

Suddenly Aang came sledding into the village on the back of a penguin.

"Looking for me?" he said to Zuko.

"You're the Avatar?" Zuko said with amazement.

Aang? The Avatar? Was that possible?

Aang agreed to go with Zuko if he spared our

village. Zuko agreed. I couldn't believe how brave Aang was; he was willing to risk his life for us. He deserved no less from me.

"Aang saved our tribe," I told Sokka and Gran Gran. "Now I'm going to save him!"

To my shock, Sokka agreed to come with me. He surprises me sometimes. Even Gran Gran was proud of me. "Only the Avatar can save the world. Go find him, little Waterbender," she said, kissing me good-bye.

I felt proud. I also felt scared. But as Aang said, if I was to become a bender, I had to face my fears. And so Sokka and I climbed up onto Appa's back.

"What was it Aang said?" Sokka asked. "Yee-ha? Hup, hup? Yip, yip?"

That did it! Appa took off into the sky. I knew that he would fly.

It didn't take us long to catch up to Prince Zuko's ship. When we did, Aang and the prince were exchanging Firebending and Airbending blows on the deck. I looked down from Appa's back in horror and saw Zuko knock Aang overboard with a fierce Firebending blast. Aang disappeared beneath the waves.

But then Aang suddenly reappeared, rising out of the ocean and riding a huge column of water! He bent the tower of water toward the deck of Zuko's ship, where it crashed down as a giant wave, knocking the prince and his soldiers into the sea. I couldn't believe my eyes!

"Now that's what I call Waterbending!" Sokka shouted.

Aang landed on the watery deck. Appa drifted down beside him, and we helped Aang climb onto Appa's back, then took off again.

"How did you do that?" I asked. "It was the most amazing Waterbending I've ever seen!"

"I don't know," Aang said. "I just sort of . . . did it."

"Why didn't you tell us that you were the Avatar?" I asked.

"Because I never wanted to be," Aang replied, turning away.

"But the world's been waiting for the Avatar to return and put an end to this war," I explained.

"And how am I going to do that?" Aang asked.

"Well, according to legend, you need to first master Waterbending, then Earthbending, then Firebending, right?" I asked.

"That's what the monks told me," Aang said.

"Well, if we go to the North Pole, you can learn Waterbending!" I suggested.

"We can learn it together," said Aang, smiling. I turned and looked at Sokka, feeling proud of him. "And Sokka, maybe you'll get to knock some Firebenders' heads along the way." I didn't want him to feel left out.

"I'd really like that," he said.

"Then we're all in this together," I said. And we headed off for the North Pole. I didn't know what the future held. Would I really learn to master Waterbending? Would Sokka become a great warrior like our father? Would Aang be able to save the world? Whatever happened, I was sure glad that I had Sokka and Aang by my side.

The Water Tribes and Their Philosophy

The Water Tribes are a peaceful people. They strive to live in harmony with nature and with the other nations of the world. There are two sects of the Water Tribes, the Northern and the Southern. In the time since the Fire Nation's attack began, contact between the two tribes has ended.

Waterbenders use their abilities for defense, never for aggression. Despite their peaceful nature, their current goal is to do whatever it takes to stop the Fire Nation from taking over the world.

WATER TRIBES' INSIGNIA

The symbol of the Water Tribes is a circle containing a crescent moon and ocean waves. The insignia represents the Moon Spirit and the Ocean Spirit, who give the Water Tribes their life and power and guide their beliefs. They coexist in harmony, the moon's force exerting a pushing and pulling motion on the ocean's water. This pushing and pulling is the foundation for the art of Waterbending. The Water Tribes' belief in peaceful cooperation among all nations stems from the relationship between these two spirits.

WATER TRIBE LEADERS

Each village in the Southern Water Tribe has its own leader, all of whom are male. The southernmost village of the Water Tribe was led by a great warrior named Hakoda, but he and the other men went off to war two years ago. Hakoda is Sokka and Katara's father. The Northern Water Tribe is ruled by Chief Arnook, a great warrior.

ARNOOK

HAKODA

SEASON

Each of the four nations is influenced by a dominant season. The Water Tribes' dominant season is winter. More Waterbenders are born during winter than during any other season.

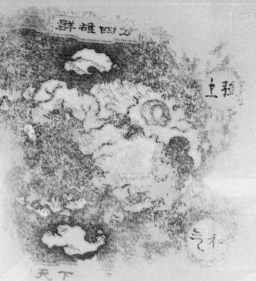

LOCATION

The Southern Water Tribe is located at the South Pole and the Northern Water Tribe at the North Pole.

In both locations the terrain is mostly ice. The weather is cold and harsh, with snow falling year-round.

NATURAL RESOURCES/FOOD

Living at the frozen poles—near the seas—the Water Tribes depend on the oceans for many of their natural resources. Sea prunes, which they serve stewed, are a favorite delicacy. Sea squid is a popular food that can be made into a variety of things, including sea squid soup. Seaweed can be used to make seaweed bread, seaweed soup, or seaweed sprinkles to top seaweed cookies. Giant sea crabs are a delicacy, considered by many to be the most delicious food in the Northern Sea.

Skins from seals are used to build tents, and pelts from polar bears cover the floors. Hunters from the Southern Water Tribe and fishermen of the Northern Water Tribe are some of the best in the world.

ANIMALS

The otter–penguin, a half–otter, half–penguin native of the South Pole, is clumsy on land but a very strong swimmer. Another animal found at both poles is the turtle–seal, which has a shell like a turtle and flippers like a seal. It slithers across the ice on its belly, then dives into openings in the ice to swim through the underwater ice tunnels. It dines on fish, shellfish, and squid. Its hard shell protects it from predators such as the polar leopard. The buffalo–yak is native to the North Pole and is a domestic animal used for transportation and carrying supplies. Because it can survive even in the coldest temperatures, the buffalo–yak is the perfect animal to take on long hunting trips into the frozen tundra. Other artic animals include polar sea lions, penguin fish, and ice crawlers.

OTTER-PENGUIN

POLAR
SEA LION

PENGUIN
FISH

THE ART OF
WATERBENDING

PHILOSOPHY AND STYLE

Waterbending is an ancient art unique to the culture of the Water Tribes. Legend says that the moon was the first Waterbender, and that ancestors of current benders saw how it pushed and pulled the ocean tides, and then learned how to control the water themselves.

Unlike the other bending arts, Waterbending is defensive in nature. Waterbenders get their strength from the spirit of the moon and their life from the spirit of the ocean. Together, they create and maintain a balance.

ANCIENT MARTIAL ARTS INFLUENCE

Waterbending is influenced by the ancient martial art of Tai Chi, which uses similar techniques to redirect the energy from an attack to use against an opponent. As with Tai Chi, the Waterbender's intent is to control opponents, not harm them. Both disciplines were influenced by ancient healing practices in which healers redirected energy paths in the body to cure ailments. Their strict belief in controlling rather than destroying; healing rather than harming; and using their power for defense, not attack, are at the heart of the humane and noble characteristics of all Waterbenders. Both Waterbending and Tai Chi are less about strength than about body alignment, breath, and visualization. In both of these arts, softness and breathing prove more powerful than hard aggression.

FORMS OF THE ELEMENT

A Waterbender can control water in any of its forms—as a liquid (water), a solid (ice or snow), or a gas (steam), including moisture in the air and ground. This gives the Waterbender a variety of defensive moves.

冰   水   雾

ICE   WATER   STEAM

WATERBENDING TECHNIQUES

Waterbenders have many techniques at their disposal. They can suspend a body of water around themselves, then lash out with water whips and powerful waves. They can stop an attacker by encasing his or her feet in ice, or escape from an opponent by creating a screen of steam for cover.

If there is no nearby body of water at the scene of a battle—such as a river, lake, or ocean—an expert Waterbender has the ability to collect all the available moisture in the air and ground around him or her. The Waterbender can then concentrate this small amount of water into a quantity that he or she can use to attack or defend.

STRENGTHS

A Waterbender's power comes from an internal life energy, which is known as chi. Because of this, a Waterbender's power is related to his or her emotional state. When a less-experienced Waterbender gets angry, his or her Waterbending force increases in intensity, but control is lost. This can be dangerous, especially in a bender with little or no training.

Waterbenders are most powerful at night, when the moon is full, when they are near their homelands of the North and South Poles, and during the winter. They can choose how to direct their energy using two *jings*, or techniques, representing the push and pull of the moon on the tides and, in turn, the push and pull of the Waterbender on the water he or she controls.

WEAKNESS

One weakness of Waterbending is the possibility that a Waterbender could find him— or herself in a place where no water can be found. This is much more probable than an Earthbender winding up without earth, or an Airbender without air. Firebenders create their own fire from the heat around them. Therefore, needing to be near a source of water is an important weakness to remember. In case there is not enough moisture in the air or ground, Waterbenders always carry skins filled with water.

HEALING

Waterbenders can use their abilities to heal by surrounding a sick or injured person with water, which then glows with a brilliant, silver-colored light. The Waterbender uses water to open chi paths in the body and help the healing process, making the person well again.

CHI

氣

THE WATER SCROLL

The legends of the Water Tribes state that long ago,
pirates stole a valuable scroll from a Waterbender of the
Northern Water Tribe. The parchment contained several
ancient Waterbending techniques, including the single
water whip, which some believed was lost forever, but
was recently recovered by a young Waterbender. As
illustrated in the scroll, the single water whip is achieved
by executing several moves. First the Waterbender
reaches forward and, with a slow stretching movement
of the arms and keeping the knees bent, draws a small
amount of water from a source. Suspending the water in
a circle in midair, the bender then slowly moves both arms
to one side of the body. This move reshapes the water,
elongating it into the form of a whip, which is unleashed
with a swift but fluid move of the arms back across
the body. The water whip follows the movement of the
Waterbender's arms, snapping like a whip.

Bato of the Water Tribes
LEGEND 2

My name is Sokka. I'm a warrior from the Southern Water Tribe. I'm not a Waterbender, like my sister, Katara, or an Airbender, like our friend Aang—who just happens to be the Avatar—but I do all right for myself. I'm pretty tough in a fight, especially against those Fire Nation jerks.

Aang, Katara, and I are traveling to the Northern Water Tribe so the two of them can learn Waterbending from a master. I'm going along to protect them and to kick a little Fire Nation butt along the way. One day, on our journey to the North Pole, we stopped on a beach to rest.

32

"Hey, look at this sword made from a whale's tooth," Aang said, picking the weapon up off the ground.

"This is a Southern Water Tribe weapon," I said, my heart racing. The warriors of my village carried these swords when they set off to battle the Fire Nation.

Then, on the nearby shore, we spotted one of their ships!

"Is this Dad's boat?" Katara asked, teary eyed.

"No," I explained. "But it is from his fleet. That means that Dad was here!"

This was as close to my father as I'd been since he left two years ago. I couldn't believe we had missed him. Maybe we'd catch up to him? Thinking about seeing him again made me so happy, but also nervous. Would he let me go to war with him now?

Or would he say I'm still too young? And what about Aang and Katara? I promised I'd help them get to the North Pole. Would I have to choose between the two?

That night we built a fire near the boat. I stared into the flames to try to take my mind off the painful memory of saying good-bye to my father, but I couldn't help thinking about the last time I saw him. I wanted to go off to war with him so badly. I had even applied traditional wolf battle paint. But my father said I was too young, and then he said something else that I never forgot: "Being a man means knowing where you are needed most. And right now that is here, protecting your sister."

I didn't understand it then, but I think I do now. I used to think that being a man meant putting on war paint, grabbing a weapon, and fighting the enemy. In the time since my father left and I've been charged with helping to protect my village, I've realized that I was

right where my people needed me most. Just like now, when Aang and Katara need me, this is where I have to be.

A sudden rustling sound snapped me back to the present. Someone was moving through the woods.

"Who's there!?" I yelled. Then, like he had stepped out of a dream, Bato, a warrior from my tribe, walked up to the fire.

"Bato!" I cried. Katara woke up.

"Sokka, Katara!" Bato said. "It is good to see you. You've both grown so much."

"Where's Dad?" I asked.

"He and the other warriors should be in the eastern Earth Kingdom by now," Bato explained. My heart sank when I heard that. I had hoped he would be here too. Bato told us that my dad brought him to this abbey after he got wounded and that the sisters have cared for him ever since.

"What smells so good?" Katara asked.

"The sisters here craft ointments and perfumes," Bato explained.

"Perfume?" I asked, never one to pass up an opportunity to crack a joke. "Maybe we can dump some on Appa! Because he stinks so much! Am I right?"

For some reason nobody laughed.

"I see you have your father's wit, Sokka," Bato finally said.

Wow! Bato thought I was like my father. I felt so proud at that moment, I didn't care that no one laughed at my joke!

After introductions, Bato invited us to his quarters. They were amazing! He lived in a cottage that looked exactly like the inside of a Southern Water Tribe hut!

"It looks like home!" Katara cried.

"Right down to the animal pelts on the floor," I added.

Then Katara spotted a bowl of stewed sea prunes over the fire. My father could eat a whole barrel of stewed sea prunes—and so could we! Over a steaming bowl of food, Bato, Katara, and I laughed and laughed about stories of home and of when my father was young.

The only weird thing was Aang interrupting our stories with dumb comments and fidgeting around the hut. I didn't know what had gotten into him.

"I have to tell you," Bato said after finishing a story, "that I'm expecting a message from your father telling me where to meet him. If you'd like, you can come along."

That was the best news I'd ever heard! I could go with Bato, join the other warriors, and fight beside my father. But then I remembered Aang.

"That would be great, Bato, but we really need to get Aang to the North Pole," I explained.

"We promised," Katara added.

"I'm sure your father would understand," Bato said. "And he would be proud that his children are helping the Avatar."

That's when Aang walked back into the hut. To be honest I hadn't even noticed he was gone. After we finished eating, Bato led us down to his ship.

"This ship has great sentimental value to me," Bato said. "It was built by my father, and he took me ice dodging in it. How was your first time ice dodging, Sokka?"

The question hit me hard. I was so embarrassed. How could I think I had become a man when I never even got to go ice dodging with my father?

"Sokka never got to go ice dodging," Katara explained. "Dad left before he was old enough."

"What's ice dodging?" Aang asked.

"It's a rite of passage for young Water Tribe members," Bato explained. "Say, I have an idea!"

And believe it or not,

Bato took me ice dodging on his ship! Aang and Katara came along too, but I was in charge. It was my turn to prove I was a man. Only, there was no ice on this river, so we dodged tall, jagged rocks.

I steered and called the shots, and Aang and Katara followed my every order. I commanded that ship like I owned it—and boy, it was a wild ride! We zoomed in between and around the sharp rocks until we came to a bunch of rocks so close together that they blocked our path. We couldn't go around them, but we sure could go over them!

"Aang, I'm going to need air in that sail!" I ordered. "Katara, I want you to bend as much water as you can between us and those rocks. Now!"

I knew exactly how to get past the obstacle. The extra air Aang shot into the sails and the wave of water Katara created lifted us up and over the rocks. We landed safely on the other side.

Bato was very proud. When we reached shore, he honored us by placing traditional tribal markings onto our foreheads with his thumb. I got the mark of the wise, the same mark my father earned during his ice dodging. I never felt prouder. I just wish Dad had been here to see it.

Then Bato gave Katara the mark of the brave, and Aang the mark of the trusted. But Aang looked away, then wiped the symbol off his forehead.

"You can't trust me," Aang said, lowering his head.

Then he reached into his pocket and pulled out a map—a map that a messenger had delivered, showing where to meet our father.

I was furious! Aang had betrayed us. I didn't understand how he could do such a thing, but I felt like I never wanted to see him again! I had to say something.

"You had the map all this time and you didn't tell us!" I yelled. "Aang, how could you?"

"I'm sorry," Aang said. "I was afraid you'd leave me."

"Well, you were right!" I screamed. "You can go to the North Pole on your own. I'm going to find Dad! Katara, are you with me?"

"I'm with you, Sokka," she replied, turning her back on Aang.

Sometimes my sister can be a real pain, but she never lets her family down. As much as she liked Aang, I'm glad she chose to come with me.

Bato led Katara and me through the forest. I was excited about seeing Dad again, but I just couldn't stop thinking about Aang. The more I walked, the more I realized that no matter what Aang had done, he needed us. Then I recalled my father's words: "Being a man means knowing where you are needed most."

"Katara, we have to go back to Aang," I said. "I want to see Dad, but helping Aang is where we're needed most."

"You're right, Sokka," Katara agreed.

"I know your father will be proud of you," Bato said.

We said our good-byes and headed off to find Aang.

Suddenly a huge beast burst from the forest, snorting and growling. The creature had light-brown fur with a dark-brown stripe running along its back. Its long tail whipped back and forth menacingly. Its enormous jaws opened to reveal razor-sharp teeth. On the beast's back rode Prince Zuko, his uncle, and some girl. The weird thing was, it seemed as if it was the girl who was controlling the beast's reins.

"Where is the Avatar?" Zuko demanded.

"We split up," I replied. "He's long gone."

"How stupid do you think I am?" Zuko asked.

"Pretty stupid," I said. Hey, the guy asked! Then Katara and I ran, but the beast charged toward us and stuck its gross, long tongue out and licked me. Within a few seconds the whole world began spinning, and then everything went black.

I woke up in the courtyard of the abbey. Katara was on the ground next to me, but neither of us could move. In front of me I watched as Zuko battled Aang and the beast fought Appa. Before each move it made, the beast sniffed around like it was searching for a scent. I figured out that the beast was able to see by using its sense of smell and decided to give it something to look at.

I asked the abbey sisters to roll out barrels of their perfume. Once we were able to move again, I smashed the barrels open with my war club and Katara Waterbended a huge wave of perfume right onto the beast.

Overwhelmed by the smells, the beast began lashing out wildly with its tongue. It struck Zuko and the girl, sending them both tumbling to the ground.

Katara and I joined Aang on Appa, and we flew off.

"So, where should we go?" Aang asked.

"To the North Pole," Katara said.

"But don't you want to see your father?" Aang asked.

"Of course we do, Aang," I replied. "But you're our family too. And right now, you need us more." I felt kind of sad as we soared into the sky. I had come so close to seeing my father again. Still, I was proud of myself. I knew I had made the right decision. One day soon I'll see Dad, and I'm sure he'll be proud of me too.

I learned all about these aspects of Water Tribe life while visiting the North and South Poles.

A SOUTHERN WATER TRIBE HUT

The inside of a typical Southern Water Tribe's hut contains a number of animal pelts that are placed on bamboo floors. At one end of the hut a sealskin tent is set up. This is used as a sleeping chamber. Ceremonial animal headdresses, spears, and animal skins are usually displayed on the walls of the hut.

In the center of the hut sits a square fire pit, surrounded by a single line of bricks. The fire provides heat for the hut and is also used to prepare food. There are mats for sitting on all four sides of the fire pit. A stew pot, used for cooking, hangs suspended from the ceiling, hovering above the fire.

ICE DODGING:
RITE OF PASSAGE, BIRTH OF A WARRIOR

When a Water Tribe boy reaches the age of fourteen, his father takes him ice dodging. This coming-of-age rite is a boy's first step in being recognized as a true warrior of the tribe. The task of the ritual is for a boy to guide a boat through a narrow body of water filled with icebergs, which the boat must avoid.

Though there is an adult onboard, once the ritual begins, the boy is the only person who can make decisions and direct the crew. He may choose two friends to assist him, by operating the main sail and the jib (a smaller sail at the rear of the boat), but he alone is in command. His skill and judgment are what make the journey a success or a failure.

If the boy is successful, he and his crew receive marks of the warrior, applied with cuttlefish paint. The mark of the wise is given for leadership ability and achievement in decision making under pressure. The mark of the brave is given for inspirational displays of courage. And the mark of the trusted is given to outsiders who prove themselves worthy of other people's trust.

MARK OF THE BRAVE

MARK OF THE WISE

MARK OF THE TRUSTED

The final tale is recounted to us by the Avatar himself, about his arrival at the North Pole and the terrible assault by the Fire Nation on the Northern Water Tribe.

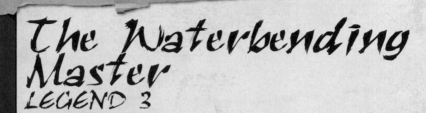

The Waterbending Master
LEGEND 3

48

My name is Aang. I'm the Avatar. At least, I'm the kid that the Avatar spirit was reborn into. I haven't mastered all of the elements yet. That's why my friends, Sokka and Katara, and I are traveling on my flying bison, Appa, to the North Pole. Katara and I both need to find a Waterbending master there in the Northern Water Tribe to teach us.

One day we were flying high above the ocean, with no land in sight, when huge chunks of ice shot out from the water!

"Look, they're Waterbenders!" Katara cried. "We've found the Northern Water Tribe!"

The city of the Northern Water Tribe was so amazing! It was way bigger than Sokka and Katara's Water Tribe village at the South Pole. That was just a bunch of ice huts, but this place looked like it was home to a pretty advanced culture. It had a really neat canal system operated by Waterbenders that moved big boats up from the sea and into the city. I was sure we'd find a master here to teach us.

Chief Arnook, leader of the Northern Water Tribe, threw a big celebration in our honor that night.

"Tonight we welcome our brother and sister from the Southern Tribe," the chief announced. "And they have brought with them the Avatar."

Everyone cheered. I waved and bowed, but I felt kind of silly doing it. After all, I still had a lot to learn about being the Avatar. We also met the chief's daughter, Princess Yue. Sokka liked her—a lot!

The chief then introduced me to Master Pakku, a great Waterbender who would become our teacher.

Early the next morning Katara and I headed for Master Pakku's training field.

"I've been waiting for this day my whole life!" Katara said.

I was excited too, though I could have used a few more hours of sleep! But when we arrived at Master Pakku's the next morning, I got the shock of my life.

"Here in the north, it is forbidden for women to learn Waterbending," he announced. "Women learn from Yagoda how to use their Waterbending for healing purposes, not for battling."

Katara was upset, and I was really annoyed. This wasn't fair! If Master Pakku wasn't going to teach Katara, then he wouldn't teach me either. I was ready to walk away and forget the whole thing. But Katara was wonderful, as usual. She reminded me how important it was for me to learn Waterbending so I could save the world. It's just like her to think first about what's best for everyone else, even when her own heart was breaking. She's the sweetest girl I've ever met!

Anyway, I agreed to start my training, and boy, was Master Pakku a tough teacher. I tried really hard to do what he said, but he was always criticizing me.

That night Sokka asked me how Waterbending training was going. I was still really upset about what Master Pakku did to Katara. Sokka suggested that I teach Katara what I learn from Master Pakku, which was a brilliant idea! At least I thought it was, until Master Pakku caught me doing it. He said I disrespected him and was no longer welcome as his student.

Well, Katara went straight to Chief Arnook, who said Master Pakku might take me back if Katara apologized to him. So she went to see him. Like I said, she is the sweetest girl. To go to all that trouble for me! But then Master Pakku called her a little girl, so she challenged him to a battle! When Katara believes in something, there's no stopping her!

Turns out that Master Pakku was very impressed with her fighting skills. And get this: Once long ago, he was in love with her grandmother! Master Pakku finally agreed to train Katara, and we were able to study together—just what I wanted.

Right when I was about as happy as I could ever remember, the Fire Nation attacked the Northern Water Tribe! I hadn't been there to help when the Fire Nation attacked my people, but this time I vowed to stop the Fire Nation!

They launched flaming boulders at the Northern Water Tribe's outer walls. I leaped onto Appa, and we flew down to their ship. I destroyed their catapults one by one and stopped their boulders. Even Appa helped!

By the time I returned to my friends, I was exhausted.

"I must have destroyed a dozen Fire Nation ships," I told them. "But there's just too many. I can't fight them all!"

"You can do a lot more than fight, Aang," Katara said. She always believes in me, even when I don't believe in myself. And she makes me feel like I'm special, not because I'm the Avatar, but just because I'm Aang.

Princess Yue told me that the Waterbenders get their strength from the moon and the ocean. I thought

that if I could contact the Moon and Ocean Spirits, they might be able to help us.

Princess Yue took Katara and me to the water oasis, the center of all spiritual energy in their land. I sat quietly and meditated in front of a koi pond, trying my best to reach the spirit world. In the pond a black fish and a white fish circled each other, again and again. I focused on the two fish, concentrating on trying to get into the spirit world.

After a few moments my tattoos began glowing, and I felt the weird sliding sensation that I always felt before crossing over. The spirit world looked like a creepy jungle, which I slowly moved through. Looking down into a pond, I was shocked to see not my own face, but the face of Avatar Roku, who was the Avatar before me. I asked him where I could find the Ocean and Moon Spirits.

"The ocean and moon are ancient spirits," Avatar Roku told me. "Long ago they crossed over into the mortal world, taking mortal forms. You must speak with the ancient spirit, Koh. He can help you."

This Koh guy was really weird and dangerous. Avatar Roku told me that if I showed any emotion, Koh would steal my face! I like my face. I'd like to keep it around for a while, so I was very careful. Koh told me that the Moon and Ocean Spirits were actually the black-and-white koi from the pond, and that someone was

trying to kill them. I had to stop that from happening.

I returned from the spirit world only to discover that my body had been taken by Prince Zuko. But Katara and Sokka showed up on Appa and rescued me. I don't know where I'd be without them. They put themselves in danger for me, and I know I'll never reach my full potential as the Avatar without their help. And they're pretty good in a fight, too! Katara has really become an amazing Waterbender, and she kicked Zuko's butt and knocked him out!

I knew that Zuko would die if we left him as he was, but even Prince Zuko doesn't deserve that. So we put him on Appa and took him with us. Then we hurried back to the oasis. There, a Fire Nation admiral named Zhao had stolen the white koi—the Moon Spirit. The moon burned a dark red and the Waterbenders grew weak.

"Destroying the moon won't just hurt the Water Tribes, Zhao!" I argued. "It will hurt everyone, even you. Without the moon, everything will fall out of balance." Even Zuko's uncle, Iroh, agreed with me. I guess sometimes I can show wisdom as the Avatar.

But Zhao turned around and shot a fireball into the pond anyway, destroying the fish! At that moment the moon vanished completely from the sky!

A great anger rose within me. I was not going to let the Fire Nation win! I was not going to let the world end this way! I waded out into the pond, focusing all my energy on the black fish that swam in a lonely circle by itself. My eyes and tattoos began to glow, and I felt myself slip into the Avatar state.

I touched the black koi—the Ocean Spirit—and merged with it to form the Ocean Spirit Monster. We became one being, made of water and light, built from the anger of the ocean in physical form. Because I was

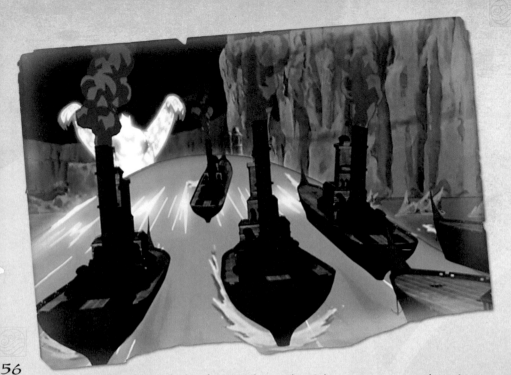

in the Avatar state, I could control the movements of the Ocean Spirit Monster, and together we were unstoppable! We used Waterbending to create huge tidal waves, which wiped out the Fire Nation's ships.

I came back to the oasis and fell out of the Avatar state. The black koi shrank to its normal size and returned to the pond.

Then a really sad thing happened.

Princess Yue gave life back the Moon Spirit. Yue was born sick, and the Moon Spirit had given her life. Now that the Moon Spirit was sick, Yue decided to give her life back to the moon. After touching the dead white koi, Yue floated into the sky, and the moon returned to its place among the stars. The white koi came back to life too, joining the black koi in their endless circle. But Princess Yue was gone.

Chief Arnook was proud of the princess, but also sad. Sokka was sad too. I was glad that I was able to help save the Northern Water Tribe. And I was very thankful for my two great friends, Sokka and Katara. Wherever my travels would now take me, I was really glad that they'd be by my side.

Especially Katara!

The Water Tribes of the North and South

Originally the southern and northern tribes lived as one at the North Pole. Following civil unrest, a group of warriors, Waterbenders, and healers

58

left to start a new tribe at the South Pole. From that time on, the two tribes evolved very differently. Before the Fire Nation War, the Southern Water Tribe lived in a beautiful, bustling city built out of the ice by Waterbenders. It was destroyed by the war, and since so many Waterbenders died fighting, the art of Waterbending practically disappeared because there were no trainers left. The Southern Water Tribe split into smaller groups and scattered across the South Pole, building simple sealskin tents or igloos made of ice to live in.

The larger Northern Water Tribe lives in one
enormous city of ice, built by Waterbenders. Several
miles wide, the Northern Water Tribe was built
on the shores of the North Sea at the North Pole.
Surrounded by ice cliffs and a giant frozen tundra, the
city sits in a horseshoe—shaped cove beneath towering
white cliffs and is dominated by large temples. It has
a huge, multilevel structure built into the landscape.

To gain entry to the great city, a group of
Waterbenders must Waterbend in group formation,
which opens a curved gateway, allowing visitors to
float into the city in boats. Once inside, the vessels must
pass through a series of locks. The Waterbenders
fill each lock with water, which raises the level of the
boats. Then they bend the water out of the locks, which
lowers the crafts to the level of the city.

The city itself is connected by a series of canals. They serve as the city's "roads." In addition to its elaborate canal system, the Northern Water Tribe's city is filled with beautiful fountains and waterfalls. In the center of the city, a long set of white stairs, with towering waterfalls on either side, leads up to the temple and the Waterbending training grounds. The highest structure is the chief's temple, which stands like a monument representing strength and power. Within its hallowed halls the chief and his chieftains make important decisions about the tribe.

CUSTOMS AND CULTURE

The Water Tribes follow different customs, traditions, and rules. The people of the larger northern tribe have a greater sense of culture than their brothers and sisters from the South Pole, but along with their larger city and longer cultural history come a stricter lifestyle and a greater sense of conformity. Members of Water Tribes participate in coming-of-age rituals. When girls in the Northern Water Tribe reach the age of sixteen, they already have arranged marriages to boys. The match and ceremony are arranged by their parents, after which the groom-to-be gives his future bride a betrothal necklace.

As you already know, when boys in the Southern Water Tribe reach the age of fourteen, they participate in the rite of passage known as ice dodging. In the Northern Water Tribe, only boys and men can train to be Waterbenders. Girls and women who have Waterbending abilities are taught to use their skills only for healing, never for fighting.

Although the members of the Southern Water Tribe live a more simple kind of life, they tend to be more open-minded. They allow girls and women to train as Waterbenders and do not force girls to enter into arranged marriages at the age of sixteen, like they do in the north. They are free to marry whomever they choose.

Epilogue

AND SO AS I WRITE

my closing and then seal this scroll, the Fire Nation
War rages on. The Northern Water Tribe has
just survived a massive attack by the Fire Nation's
fleet, thanks to the Avatar and the Ocean Spirit.
Prince Zuko of the Fire Nation is considered an
outcast by his father, the Fire lord. He is continuing his
quest to find the Avatar, traveling not on a powerful
Fire Nation ship, but on a small wooden raft.
Master Pakku, the Waterbending master of the
northern kingdom, along with other Waterbenders,
has set out for the South Pole. They hope to
help rebuild the Southern Water Tribe.
Aang will now learn Waterbending from
Katara, who is on her way to becoming a
Waterbending master. Sokka, Katara, and Aang
have set off on Appa to journey to the Earth
Kingdom. There, Aang hopes to find a master
to teach him Earthbending as he continues his
journey to fulfill his destiny as the Avatar.
Now you know all that I can tell you so far.
Please show this only to those whom you would
trust with your life. I must ask you to keep these
sacred scrolls safe and hidden from prying eyes. The
knowledge you have gained is a powerful tool, and
the fate of four nations now depends on you. . . .